Froggo

by Penny Dolan and Marco Lombardini

Once there was an enormous house in a big garden.

In the garden, there was a pond.

In the pond, there lived some frogs.

The frogs swam in the cool, deep water.

They slept in the soft, dark mud.

They sat on the lily-pads and listened to
Old Frog's stories.

"Long ago," said Old Frog with a croak, "a beautiful princess lost her golden ball in this very pond. A handsome frog got it back. So she kissed him ..."

"And then what happened?" called the frogs. But they already knew what happened next.

"He turned into a prince. He lived in a beautiful palace and sat on a golden throne."

"Hooray!" shouted all the frogs.

They loved to hear the story.

But not Froggo.

"Boring," said Froggo to himself.

"I would not like to be a prince.

I want to be a footballer

and run and jump and play,

not sit on a throne all day."

One hot afternoon, Froggo was sitting under the cool reeds when he saw some children. They were running across the grass, laughing and playing football.

Suddenly, the ball bounced too far and fell into the water.
Froggo saw the ball land in his pond.

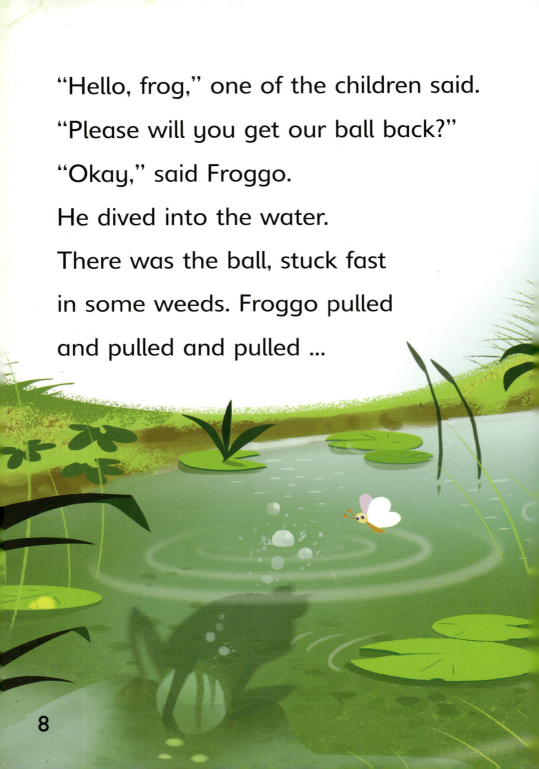

"Hello, frog," one of the children said.

"Please will you get our ball back?"

"Okay," said Froggo.

He dived into the water.

There was the ball, stuck fast

in some weeds. Froggo pulled

and pulled and pulled ...

... until at last the ball was free!
Froggo swam back up with the ball
and threw it high up into the air.

The ball landed on the grass
and bounced away.
Some of the children chased after it.
But one little girl stayed and watched
as Froggo swam up and sat back on
a lily-pad.
"Thank you, little frog," she said.

She bent her head and kissed him
on the tip of his nose.
Froggo began to feel funny
and everything began to spin.

There was a flash of light and suddenly there stood a tall, strong footballer, wearing a football kit and boots.

"Wow!" said Froggo, jumping for joy.

The little girl gave him a big smile.
"You are great at jumping!
Would you like to play football
with us? You could play in goal."
"Oh, yes please," said Froggo.

From that day on, Froggo the Footballer was happy.

Every day he played football with the children. Everyone loved to watch him jumping and saving goals.

And now, whenever Old Frog sits on his log, he has a new story to tell.

A story about a young frog who did not want to be a prince.

Story order

Look at these 5 pictures and captions.
Put the pictures in the right order
to retell the story.

1

Froggo got the children's ball back.

2

Froggo turned into a footballer.

3

Froggo found Old Frog's story boring.

4

The little girl kissed Froggo.

5

The children played football near the pond.

Guide for Independent Reading

This series is designed to provide an opportunity for your child to read on their own. These notes are written for you to help your child choose a book and to read it independently.

In school, your child's teacher will often be using reading books which have been banded to support the process of learning to read. Use the book band colour your child is reading in school to help you make a good choice. *Froggo* is a good choice for children reading at Turquoise Band in their classroom to read independently.

The aim of independent reading is to read this book with ease, so that your child enjoys the story and relates it to their own experiences.

About the book

Froggo thinks being turned into a prince would be boring. So when a little girl kisses him on the nose, he becomes a footballer instead!

Before reading

Help your child to learn how to make good choices by asking:
"Why did you choose this book? Why do you think you will enjoy it?"
Look at the cover together and ask: "What do you think the story will be about?" Ask your child to think of what they already know about the story context. Then ask your child to read the title aloud.
Ask: "What do you think Froggo will be doing in the story?"
Remind your child that they can sound out a word in syllable chunks if they get stuck.
Decide together whether your child will read the story independently or read it aloud to you.

During reading

Remind your child of what they know and what they can do independently. If reading aloud, support your child if they hesitate or ask for help by telling the word. If reading to themselves, remind your child that they can come and ask for your help if stuck.

After reading

Support comprehension by asking your child to tell you about the story. Use the story order puzzle to encourage your child to retell the story in the right sequence, in their own words. The correct sequence can be found on the next page.

Help your child think about the messages in the book that go beyond the story and ask: "Do you think Froggo will ever want to be a frog again? What do you think his frog friends think of him when he becomes a footballer?"

Give your child a chance to respond to the story: "Did you have a favourite part? What did you think would happen when the little girl kissed Froggo the frog?"

Extending learning

Help your child understand the story structure by using the same sentence patterning and adding different elements. "Let's make up a new story about Froggo. What else might Froggo have dreamed about turning into? How about a superhero or a pop star, or even a different animal, such as a lion or dragon?"

In the classroom, your child's teacher may be teaching about recognising punctuation marks. Ask your child to identify some question marks and exclamation marks in the story and then ask them to practise reading the whole sentences with appropriate expression.

Franklin Watts
First published in Great Britain in 2020
by The Watts Publishing Group

Copyright © The Watts Publishing Group 2020
All rights reserved.

Series Editors: Jackie Hamley and Melanie Palmer
Series Advisors: Dr Sue Bodman and Glen Franklin
Series Designers: Peter Scoulding and Cathryn Gilbert

A CIP catalogue record for this book is
available from the British Library.

ISBN 978 1 4451 6875 3 (hbk)
ISBN 978 1 4451 6876 0 (pbk)
ISBN 978 1 4451 6877 7 (library ebook)

Printed in China

Franklin Watts
An imprint of
Hachette Children's Group
Part of The Watts Publishing Group
Carmelite House
50 Victoria Embankment
London EC4Y 0DZ

An Hachette UK Company
www.hachette.co.uk

www.reading-champion.co.uk

FSC
www.fsc.org
MIX
Paper from
responsible sources
FSC® C104740

Answer to Story order: 3, 5, 1, 4, 2